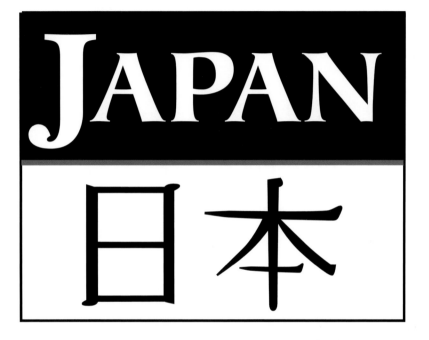

JAPAN
日本

Written by Ena Keo

STECK-VAUGHN
COMPANY
ELEMENTARY · SECONDARY · ADULT · LIBRARY

Contents

Beautiful Islands 3

Living in Japan 4

Japanese People...............12

Festivals in Japan 18

Where the Sun Began.......22

Glossary 24

Index 25

Beautiful Islands

Thousands of years ago, there was a giant **volcano** in the Pacific Ocean. It formed a group of four **islands.** These islands make up the country of Japan. It is one of the most interesting and beautiful countries in the world.

Living in Japan

There are many cities in Japan. The largest is Tokyo. It is the **capital** of Japan. Tokyo is a very **modern** city. Its streets are filled with large buildings, restaurants, and shops.

Tokyo is also a very crowded city. Most people living there have a small apartment. They visit parks and gardens for outdoor fun.

Few people live outside of Japan's cities. But some do live on small farms. Most Japanese farmers grow rice or tea. Others grow fruits or vegetables.

Farm life in Japan is not as modern as city life. Japanese farmers often do their work in the fields by hand.

Japanese houses are small. They usually have one to four rooms. The rooms have low tables with mats around them where people sit. Some walls are really sliding doors made of paper.

All Japanese people take off their shoes before going into their homes. In Japan, wearing outdoor shoes inside a house is bad manners.

The streets in Japanese cities are crowded with cars. Still, many people do not own a car. For short trips, they ride bikes or trains. For longer trips, Japanese people often ride bullet trains. Bullet trains move very fast as they speed from city to city.

Japanese People

Japanese people like to eat fish, rice, and vegetables every day. They like food to be very fresh. Sometimes they even eat fish raw.

When Japanese people eat, they do not usually use forks, spoons, and knives. Instead, they eat their food with **chopsticks.**

Japanese handwriting is very beautiful. It looks like small pictures. The pictures stand for words. Japanese children spend many hours learning to write.

Japanese is the **language** spoken by everyone. Today many people in Japan speak English, too.

Japanese children go to school nearly every day. They even go on Saturdays. But they do not go to school in the summer.

Summertime is when most Japanese families take their vacations. Many people go to the beach. Or they visit family members who live far away.

Festivals in Japan

There are many **festivals** in Japan. They are celebrated with dances and music. Japanese people wear **kimonos** during festivals. Kimonos are robes made of colorful silk or cotton. Even children wear them!

The biggest festival is held on New Year's Day. On this day, Japanese people visit friends and family. They exchange gifts and eat a special meal together.

The Kite Festival has been held in Japan for 400 years. During this festival, people fly huge, colorful kites high in the sky.

Where the Sun Began

Japan is called *Nippon.* This means "where the sun began." That is why there is a large red sun on the Japanese flag. Japanese people are very proud of their beautiful country.

Glossary

capital main city in a country

chopsticks wooden sticks used for eating

festivals celebrations for a special time

islands land surrounded on all sides by water

kimonos long, loose robes

language words spoken and written

modern new

volcano mountain that has hot rock inside